A BAND OF
JOINING-IN STORIES

Also available from Pat Thomson,
and published by Doubleday/Corgi:

A BUS FULL OF STORIES FOR FOUR YEAR OLDS

A POCKETFUL OF STORIES FOR FIVE YEAR OLDS

A BUCKETFUL OF STORIES FOR SIX YEAR OLDS

A BASKET OF STORIES FOR SEVEN YEAR OLDS

A SACKFUL OF STORIES FOR EIGHT YEAR OLDS

A CHEST OF STORIES FOR NINE YEAR OLDS

A SATCHEL OF SCHOOL STORIES

A CRACKER FULL OF CHRISTMAS STORIES

A STOCKING FULL OF CHRISTMAS STORIES

A
Band of
Joining-in
Stories

Collected and arranged by Pat Thomson
Illustrated by Steve Cox

DOUBLEDAY

LONDON . NEW YORK . TORONTO . SYDNEY . AUCKLAND

TRANSWORLD PUBLISHERS LTD
61–63 Uxbridge Road, London W5 5SA

TRANSWORLD PUBLISHERS (AUSTRALIA) PTY LTD
15–25 Helles Avenue, Moorebank, NSW 2170

TRANSWORLD PUBLISHERS (NZ) LTD
3 William Pickering Drive, Albany, Auckland

DOUBLEDAY CANADA LTD
105 Bond Street, Toronto, Ontario M5B 1Y3

Published 1995 by Doubleday
a division of Transworld Publishers Ltd

A catalogue record for this book is available from the British Library

ISBN 0 385 40543X

Typeset in Monotype Bembo Schoolbook by
Phoenix Typesetting, Ilkley, West Yorkshire.

Printed in Great Britain
by Mackays of Chatham plc, Chatham, Kent.

CONTENTS

Acknowledgements

The editor and publisher are grateful for permission to include the following copyright material in this anthology:

Mary Danby Calvert, for 'The Biggest Cream Bun in the World', copyright © Mary Danby Calvert 1972.

Alice B. Coats, 'Horace', from *The Story of Horace*, © 1937. Reprinted by permission of Faber and Faber Ltd.

Wanda Gag, 'Millions of Cats'. Reprinted by permission of Faber and Faber Ltd.

Phyllis Flowerdew, 'The House by the Stream' from *More Stories for Telling*, published by Johnston and Bacon, 1968.

Every effort has been made to trace and contact copyright holders before publication. If any errors or omissions occur, the publisher will be pleased to rectify these at the earliest opportunity.

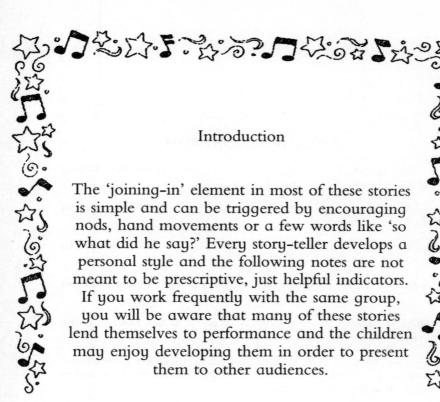

Introduction

The 'joining-in' element in most of these stories is simple and can be triggered by encouraging nods, hand movements or a few words like 'so what did he say?' Every story-teller develops a personal style and the following notes are not meant to be prescriptive, just helpful indicators. If you work frequently with the same group, you will be aware that many of these stories lend themselves to performance and the children may enjoy developing them in order to present them to other audiences.

Drat that Fat Cat!

To get the story to go with a swing, first
practise the question:

Story-teller: And was that cat fat enough?
Listeners: NO, HE WAS NOT!

The listeners have no trouble at all picking up
the rest, especially the animal noises.

Drat that Fat Cat!

Once there was a cat, a fat, fat cat. But was that cat fat enough?

NO, HE WAS NOT.

So he padded along the path in search of food.

The fat cat met a rat.
    'Have you any food, rat?'
    'No, I have not,' said the rat.
    'Too bad, then. I must eat *you* up.'
    'But you are fat enough already!'
    But was that fat cat fat enough?

NO, HE WAS NOT.

So he gobbled up the rat and padded along the path in search of food, with the rat going squeak, squeak, squeak inside him.

The fat cat met a duck.
  'Have you any food, duck?'
  'No, I have not,' said the duck.
  'Too bad, then. I must eat *you* up.'
  'But you are fat enough already!'
  But was that cat fat enough?

NO, HE WAS NOT.

So he gobbled up the duck and padded down the path in search of food with the duck going quack, quack, quack and the rat going squeak, squeak, squeak inside him.

The fat cat met a dog.
  'Have you any food, dog?'
  'No, I have not,' said the dog.
  'Too bad, then. I must eat *you* up.'
  'But you are fat enough already!'
  But was that cat fat enough?

NO, HE WAS NOT.

So he padded along the path in search
of food with the dog going woof, woof,
woof, the duck going quack, quack,
quack and the rat going squeak, squeak,
squeak inside him.

The fat cat met an old lady.
  'Have you any food, old lady?'
  'No, I have not,' said the old lady.
  'Too bad, then. I must eat *you* up.'
  'But you are fat enough already!'
  But was that cat fat enough?

NO, HE WAS NOT.

So he gobbled up the old lady and
padded along the path in search of food
with the old lady going 'Drat that fat
cat,' the dog going woof, woof, woof,
the duck going quack, quack, quack
and the rat going squeak, squeak,
squeak inside him.

A bee buzzed round the fat cat's head
and, without a thought, he swallowed it
whole.

The bee buzzed round inside the fat
cat where he found a rat going squeak,
squeak, squeak, a duck going quack,
quack, quack, a dog going woof, woof,
woof and an old lady going 'Drat that
fat cat' inside him.

'This is an outrage!' buzzed the bee.
'There isn't room to swing a cat in
here.'

The fat cat had forgotten that bees
sting.

'Ow!' cried the fat cat. 'Meeow, ow,
ow!' and he got the hiccups.

'Hic,' went the cat and out popped the bee.

'Hic,' went the cat and out popped the rat.

'Hic,' went the cat and out popped the duck.

'Hic,' went the cat and out popped the dog.

'Hic,' went the cat and out popped the old lady.

'Dear me,' said the old lady, 'what a

very thin cat. Come home with me and
I'll fatten you up.' The cat padded
along the path behind her, in search of
food, going hic, hic, hic all the way
home.

So, was that cat fat enough?

NO, HE WAS NOT!

This story is by Pat Thomson.

The Biggest Cream Bun in the World

This one is all about noise. Usually no encouragement is needed. The words 'like this' signal each noise, and if each is repeated, most listeners have it by the second time. (Indeed, they often have it quite loudly.)

The Biggest Cream Bun in the World

Big Fat Rosie was the biggest, fattest person there ever was.

She was bigger than a barrel.

She was plumper than a pudding.

She was rounder than a rubber ball.

And almost as heavy as a medium-sized hippopotamus.

And Big Fat Rosie was very, very wide. She was so wide that:

She had to sit on an extra-wide chair.

She had to sleep in an extra-wide bed.

She had to eat with an extra-wide spoon.

And all the doors in her house were extra-extra wide, so that she could move from room to room without getting stuck.

Everything that Big Fat Rosie did was done enormously. When she ate (with her extra-wide spoon), she made a noise like this:

ompa chompa ompa chompa

When she slept (in her extra-wide bed), she snored like this:

cor-fyoo cor-fyoooooo

and all the walls quivered.

When she cried, like this:

owo-WO-OWO-WO-WO

such huge tears fell from her eyes that everything around her became soaking wet.

Big Fat Rosie was a farmer's wife, and her husband was called Turnip Tom. While Rosie looked after the house, Turnip Tom managed everything around the farm. He had pigs and cows and ducks and chickens and he grew wheat, cabbages, potatoes and, of course, turnips. Turnip Tom was very good to Big Fat Rosie and bought her plenty of nice things to eat. This made Big Fat Rosie happy, because she was very greedy indeed – and her favourite food was cream buns.

One day, when Turnip Tom was out working in the fields, Big Fat Rosie thought she would give him a surprise. She would make a great big cream bun and they could eat it together for their tea. She giggled happily, like this:

Ki Ki Ki Ki

and made a list of all the things she would need: flour, eggs, milk, butter, sugar and cream.

There were big bags of flour and sugar in the larder, but the other ingredients would have to be collected from the farm.

Big Fat Rosie put on her rubber farm boots and went first to the cowshed, where Old Harry, the farm boy, was putting hay in the cows' manger. Outside, the cows made hungry, waiting noises, like this:

mooooooo moooooo moOOOOOO

'Hallo, Harry,' said Big Fat Rosie. 'Please may I have some milk and some butter and some cream? I'm going to make the biggest cream bun in the world.'

'Arr,' said Harry, scratching his head.

'When a bun's big as that, there'll be some as gets fat.'

'Yes,' agreed Rosie, laughing cosily, 'me.' (Because, of course, she was already as fat as a couple of eiderdowns.)

Harry went into the dairy and came out with a can of milk, a bowl of butter and a jug of cream. Big Fat Rosie thanked him and trotted off towards the henhouse to look for some eggs.

When the hens saw her, they made a
fearful racket, like this:

cookerookeroo cookerookeroo roo

and flapped about her feet.

'No, no!' cried Big Fat Rosie. 'It isn't
tea-time yet. I've come to fetch some
eggs.' She went over to the nesting
boxes and looked inside. There were ten
beautiful speckly-brown eggs, some of
them still warm. She put them in her

apron pocket and walked carefully back
to the farmhouse, trying not to bump
them with her knees. 'Hee hee!' she
thought. 'Now I can make the biggest
cream bun in the world!'

When the mixture was ready in the
bowl, Big Fat Rosie stirred it with her
wooden spoon, like this:

slurrrp slurrrp

and licked her lips. She tasted the
mixture twenty-six times, just to be sure
it was right, and added a few spoonfuls
of yeast. Yeast would make the bun rise
splendidly, like a loaf of bread. Turnip
Tom *would* be pleased.

Big Fat Rosie bent down to light the
oven. It made a noise like this:

pop pop

and she poured the bun mixture on to

the biggest baking tray she could find.
When she had placed it in the oven, she
sat in her very wide rocking chair and
hummed a little happy tune as she
rocked, like this:

dum di dum di dum dummety dummety dum

And then she fell asleep.
    In the oven, the bun was rising higher
and higher. In the chair, Rosie was
snoring louder and louder, like this:

cor-fyoo cor-fyooooo

The whole kitchen was shaking with the noise – until suddenly the oven door burst open with a bang. Big Fat Rosie woke up, rubbed her eyes and looked around her. What on earth was that peculiar sound? It went like this:

splobble splobble

It was the bun! It was pouring out of the oven! Over the floor it crept steadily, blobbing and bubbling, slopping and slurping.

It looked as though it would never stop. But Big Fat Rosie was not going to be beaten by a bun. She knew she could never sweep it up — but she could eat it. It was almost time for tea, anyway. She grabbed the nearest piece and began to eat very fast, like this:

ompa chompa ompa chompa

But the bun kept on coming. It was rising up the table legs and Big Fat Rosie had to eat even faster, like this:

ompa chompa ompa chompa

She wished she had never put all that yeast in the mixture.

Then the bun began to creep over the window-sill and out into the garden. Turnip Tom, coming home from the fields, called out to Harry.

'Come quick! There's a bun climbing out of the window!'

'Dearie me,' said Harry and hurried with him to the kitchen. There they found Big Fat Rosie knee deep in bun, eating more and more slowly, like this:

om-pah-chom-pah

'Omp,' she mumbled, almost in tears. 'It was going – omp – to be the biggest chomp bomp in the womp.'

'Never mind,' said Turnip Tom, who always knew exactly what to do. 'Harry and I can take it away in a barrow.'

'Arr,' said Harry.

They fetched their shovels and a wheelbarrow and began to scrape the cream bun off the walls. Harry switched off the oven and the rest of the dough began to sink.

Finally, it stopped. Turnip Tom gave a great big sigh of relief, like this:

whee~yew

and stood looking thoughtfully at the barrowload of bun. 'We could bury it in the garden,' he suggested.

Harry said: 'When a bun gets too big, remember the pig.'

So they gave the bun to Alexander, who was always hungry, and he grunted happily, like this:

oinker oinker oink

as if to say 'Thank you very much.'

But Big Fat Rosie thought he was saying, 'What a rotten cook', and decided she would make another biggest cream bun in the world tomorrow, just to show him. And this time it would be even bigger.

This story is by Mary Calvert.

The Farmer's Wife Makes the Jam

This is a very active (and somewhat hilarious) story. Every action is indicated in the story but the teller usually needs to show that everyone may join in. When you say 'and she stirred and she stirred and she stirred', listeners should be invited to copy the action and told to 'keep it up'. Each action is added to the previous one so, finally, everyone should be stirring, rocking, nodding and shooing at the same time. At this point, everyone collapses, so call 'last time' and bring it all together again with the easier last four lines, everyone saying together (and acting out) the separate actions:

Stir, stir, stir.
Rock, rock, rock.
Nod, nod, nod.
Shoo, shoo, shoo, shoo, shoo!

The Farmer's Wife Makes the Jam

One day, the farmer's wife got up very early indeed. She fluffed up the feather bed and smoothed the coverlet.

So that was done.

She took the broom and swept the floor.

So that was done.

She went outside and fed the chickens.

So that was done.

She brought the baby's cradle into the kitchen and saw that he was sleeping peacefully.

So now she was ready.

You see, today she was going to

make the jam and when you make jam you must stir and stir and stir without stopping, or the jam will burn. She put all the ingredients in the pan and she stirred and she stirred and she stirred.

(Stir the pot and keep stirring)

Wouldn't you just believe it? As soon as she had the jam bubbling in the pan, the baby woke up.

'Ssh,' she said, 'ssh, ssh.'

But it was no good. The baby began to cry. She put out her foot and began to rock the cradle.

(Rock to and fro and keep stirring)

She rocked and rocked and rocked,
And she stirred and stirred and stirred.

Oh, no! She saw Mrs Chatterbox
from next door going past the window.
There was a knock on the door and in
she swept, leaving the door wide open.
How she talked! Chatter, chatter,
chatter, and all the farmer's wife wanted
to do was to get on with making her
precious jam. She pretended to listen and
just nodded her head.

Chatter,
Chatt
Chat

(Nod head regularly, rock and keep stirring)

She nodded and nodded and nodded,
She rocked and rocked and rocked,
And she stirred and stirred and stirred.

The jam thickened. She was nearly finished now. Just a little longer.

But the farmer's wife had been in a hurry when she fed the chickens that morning and she hadn't fastened them up properly. Through the open door came all the chickens, right into the house. With her free hand, she shooed them out of the kitchen, 'Shoo, shoo, shoo!'

(Flap hand, nod, rock and keep stirring)

43

So she shooed and shooed and
shooed,
    She nodded and nodded and nodded,
    She rocked and rocked and rocked,
    And she stirred and stirred and stirred.

So this is how the farmer's wife finished
making her jam—

*(For a grand finale, at the same time stir,
rock, nod, flap hand, then abandon
everything, flap with both hands and
shout, 'Shoo, shoo, shoo, shoo, shoo!')*

Stir, stir, stir.
Rock, rock, rock,
Nod, nod, nod,
Shoo, shoo, shoo, shoo, shoo!

This story is by Pat Thomson

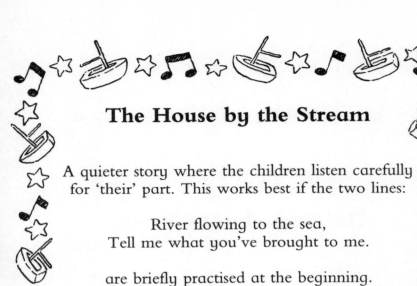

The House by the Stream

A quieter story where the children listen carefully for 'their' part. This works best if the two lines:

River flowing to the sea,
Tell me what you've brought to me.

are briefly practised at the beginning.

The House by the Stream

Franz lived in a little wooden house on the mountain-side in Switzerland. It stood by itself among the fir trees and the pines, with a great green meadow spreading in front of it, and a narrow stony road leading down to the village below. A few yards from the door of the house a little stream went splashing by, just a small stream that tumbled over the rocks and sang its song all through the day and all through the night. It started somewhere near the top of the mountain, where patches of snow lingered all through the year, and by the time it reached Franz's house it was carrying odd little twigs and bits of broken branches or fat fir cones, all bobbing along like boats. In that place one large rock lay stretched out in the water like a lazy crocodile, and everything that floated down on the stream had to stop there for a few minutes and wait till it was whirled out and taken on its way again.

Franz had a special game. He would stand on the bank and cover his eyes with his hands. Then he would say,

'River, flowing to the sea,
Tell me what you've brought for me.'

He would wait a few moments. Then he would uncover his eyes and look. He knew, of course, that it was a stream and not a river, and he knew, of course, that it would never bring anything but odd little twigs and bits of broken

branches or fat fir cones, but he always
pretended that these things were
treasures. He would poke at them with
a long stick and drag them to the bank
and catch hold of them, and say to
himself, 'Another little bag of gold.
Another little stick of silver.'

He would put them on the grass and
count them to see how many he had
found.

Now, much higher up the mountain
in a wooden hut, there lived an old man
called Arnulf. His real home was in the
village, but every summer he took his
cows up to the higher pastures and lived
up there with them. Sometimes when
he came down to the village for bread,
he stopped to chat to Franz's father
or mother. Franz was a little afraid
of him because he had such a bushy
grey beard and such a wrinkled brown
face.

One day when old Arnulf was talking
to Franz's father, he looked across at
Franz and said, 'That's a fine game,
isn't it?'

For Franz, not knowing anyone was
listening, was standing by the stream,
covering his eyes with his hands and
saying loudly,

'River, flowing to the sea,
Tell me what you've brought for me.'

51

'Yes,' said Franz's father to old Arnulf. 'Everything gets stuck by the rock there for a few minutes. Franz pulls twigs and cones out with a stick, and pretends they are treasures. It's a new game. He plays it every day, about this time, when he's tired of everything else.'

'It's the same stream that flows by my hut,' replied Arnulf. 'I'll send a real treasure down for him one day.' Franz's father laughed, and old Arnulf went trudging on his way up the mountain. Father went on with his work; and Franz went on with his game, not even knowing that Arnulf had been there at all.

That evening, when old Arnulf was sitting outside his hut, he noticed a funny twisted branch lying on the ground.

'Looks like a sea-serpent,' he said, and he took his knife and cut off a bit here and a bit there. Then he smoothed down the part that looked like a head and he carved out two eyes, and there it was, a sea-serpent made of wood!

'I'll send it down the stream to the little boy Franz tomorrow evening,' he thought. 'Maybe it will float away before he sees it, but if it doesn't, he *will* get a surprise.'

The next evening Franz stood beside the stream at the usual time. He covered his eyes with his hands and he said,

'River, flowing to the sea,
Tell me what you've brought for me.'

He waited a few moments. Then he uncovered his eyes and looked. He saw a broken twig floating towards the rock.

'One little stick of silver,' he said.

He saw two fir cones bobbing along like boats.

'Two little bags of gold,' he said.

There were some straggling stems of a green weed tangled up in the water beside the rock, and a twisted branch had drifted there too and could not get out again into the main stream.

'I'll have to set them free,' thought Franz. 'Otherwise everything will stop there and the stream will get blocked.' This did happen sometimes, so Franz took a long stick and poked at the green weed and dragged it towards the bank. Then he poked again at the twisted branch. He was just about to pull it to the bank when he stopped. *Was* it a twisted branch or was it a snake or a sea-serpent? It had a head and two eyes. It *looked* like a sea-serpent! For a moment Franz felt frightened. Then he knew at once that it could not be

anything alive, so he poked at it again
with his stick, and he pulled it ashore.

'A wooden sea-serpent!' he laughed,
and he wondered who had carved it and
dropped it into the stream. He ran to
show it to his mother and father, saying,
'The river really did bring me a treasure
today. Look! It's a sea-serpent!' Mother
and Father laughed and said how nice it
was.

'I wonder who made it,' murmured
Mother, but Father said nothing for he
knew that old Arnulf must have made it
and dropped it into the stream outside
his mountain hut.

55

Later that evening, when Franz was asleep with the wooden sea-serpent on the table beside his bed, old Arnulf sat outside his hut in the setting sun. He was chipping away at another bit of wood, quite a big bit from a broken branch. Arnulf was good at making things, and in a very short time he had made a boat.

'I'll send it down the stream to the little boy Franz tomorrow evening,' he thought. 'Maybe it will float away before he sees it, but if it doesn't, he *will* get a surprise.'

The next evening Franz stood beside the stream at the usual time. He covered his eyes with his hands and he said,

'River, flowing to the sea,
Tell me what you've brought for me.'

He waited a few moments. Then he uncovered his eyes and looked. He saw

56

two broken twigs floating towards the rock.

'Two little sticks of silver,' he said.

He saw three fir cones bobbing along like boats.

'Three little bags of gold,' he said.

Then he saw something else. He saw a little wooden boat – a toy one carved out of wood. It came sailing down the stream straight towards the large rock that stretched out in the water like a lazy crocodile. There it stopped, waiting to be whirled out and taken on its way again. Quickly Franz poked at it with his long stick, and pulled it to the bank. He lifted it out of the stream and looked at it.

'A wooden boat!' he exclaimed, and he wondered who had carved it. He ran to show it to his mother and father, saying, 'The river brought me *another* treasure today! Look! It's a toy boat.' Mother and Father looked at it and said how nice it was.

'I wonder who made it,' murmured Mother, but Father said nothing for he knew that old Arnulf must have made it and dropped it into the stream outside his mountain hut.

Later that evening when Franz was asleep, with the wooden sea-serpent and the wooden boat on the table beside his bed, Arnulf sat outside his hut in the setting sun, chipping away at another bit of wood. Arnulf was good at making things and in a very short time he had made a bear.

'I'll send it down the stream to the little boy Franz tomorrow evening,' he thought. 'Maybe it will float away

58

before he sees it, but if it doesn't he *will* get a surprise.' He stood it on a shelf in his hut – but he did not send it down the stream to Franz next day after all, because on that day something happened.

It happened at midday, when the sun was high in the sky and Arnulf's cows were grazing peacefully on the fresh mountain grass. Every time the cows moved a step or took a mouthful of grass, their cow-bells rang gently, so that all the mountain was filled with quiet little cow-bell tunes. Then suddenly Arnulf heard a loud moo. It was not an ordinary moo of contentment. It was a frightened moo. A cow was in trouble somewhere, and as she mooed, her cow-bell jangled in a nervous way too.

Old Arnulf walked across the grass and clambered down over the rocks, and there he saw the cow. She had set a

great stone loose and it had rolled
against another one and trapped her
back hoof. Really she could have moved
her hoof quite easily but she was too
frightened to do anything but moo.

'Silly old cow,' said Arnulf gently. It
took him only a moment to free her and
send her up towards the grass again, but
just then he slipped himself. He slipped
on a patch of damp moss, and though
he thought it was just an ordinary fall,

he knew as soon as he tried to stand up that it was not.

'I must have twisted my leg,' he thought, and he sank to the earth again in pain. He lay there for some time, unable to move. Then he said to himself, 'I *must* move! I *must* get back to my hut.'

Somehow, clutching at the rocks and dragging himself along the ground, he managed to reach the grass and then at last the hut. He knew by this time that his leg must be broken and he knew that he needed a doctor. But how could he get help? There was no phone. There were no houses anywhere near. No one was likely to pass that way at all. Then he noticed the wooden bear he had carved for Franz, and the bear gave him an idea.

He would paint a message on a piece of wood and send it down the stream to Franz.

'Maybe it will float away before he sees it,' he thought, 'but if it doesn't, he might get help for me.'

Arnulf had a little white paint in an old tin. He also had a flat strip of wood which he had taken down from the hut because it was worn. He had put a new strip of pine wood in its place. Now he dipped a brush into the white paint and he wrote in large letters on the old strip of wood, 'Help. Arnulf.'

That evening, Franz stood beside the stream at the usual time. He covered his eyes with his hands and he said,

'River flowing to the sea,
Tell me what you've brought for me.'

He wondered what he would find today. Yesterday he had found a boat. The day before, he had found a wooden sea-serpent. What *would* he find today? He waited a few moments. Then he uncovered his eyes and looked.

'Oh dear!' he cried, for a big strip of old, black wood had jammed itself between the rocks. It was just too long to float up to the large rock that lay stretched out in the water like a lazy crocodile, and it was stopping everything else from going there too. So odd little twigs, and broken branches and fat fir cones were all sailing straight towards the village.

'I must move *that*,' thought Franz.
'Otherwise I shall get no treasures at
all.' He poked at the strip of black wood
with his stick. He pulled at it and
pushed at it and at last he set it free.

'You go away,' he said, and he gave
it a great push towards the village. He
pushed it so hard that the strip of black
wood gave a splash and turned right
over. Then Franz saw that something

was written on it. He could not read very well, or very much, but he *could* read the large white words that said, 'Help. Arnulf.'

'Father, Father!' he called. 'Come quickly!'

Father came. He was just in time to see the words, 'Help. Arnulf,' before they floated out of sight, and at that moment Franz suddenly knew that it must have been Arnulf who had sent the wooden sea-serpent and the wooden boat down the stream.

Father and another man climbed up the mountain to Arnulf's hut. They took a stretcher with them and they carried Arnulf down as far as the road, where the doctor met them in an ambulance. Arnulf was taken to hospital, and his brother from the village had to go up to the hut and look after the cows.

Later, when Father came home again he said to Franz, 'You were a good boy, Franz. You've been a great help to Arnulf. He'll be all right now that he is being looked after in hospital.'

'Did Arnulf send the wooden sea-serpent down the stream?' asked Franz.

'Yes. He sent it for you.'

'And did he send the boat for me too?'

'Yes, he did.'

'There won't be any more real treasures then,' said Franz.

'Afraid not,' answered Father, 'not until Arnulf is better anyway.'

And when old Arnulf *was* better at the

end of the summer, and when Franz
stood by the stream once more and said,

'River, flowing to the sea,
Tell me what you've brought for me,'

– well, the first thing that came down
the stream was a wooden bear who had
been waiting in the hut high up in the
mountain all the summer long.

This story is by Phyllis Flowerdew.

Millions of Cats

The repeated chorus, the first of which starts 'Cats here, cats there,' is easily learnt without any preparation, usually line by line. First of all the children will join in with 'Millions and billions and trillions of cats' and as the story progresses, the story-teller's 'Hundreds of cats' will trigger the rest.

Millions of Cats

Once upon a time there was a very old man and a very old woman. They lived in a nice clean house which had flowers all around it, except where the door was. But they couldn't be happy because they were so very lonely.

'If we only had a cat!' sighed the very old woman.

'A cat?' asked the very old man.

'Yes, a sweet little fluffy cat,' said the very old woman.

'I will get you a cat, my dear,' said the very old man.

And he set out over the hills to look

for one. He climbed over the sunny hills. He trudged through the cool valleys. He walked a long, long time and at last he came to a hill which was quite covered with cats.

Cats here, cats there,
Cats and kittens everywhere

Hundreds of cats,
Thousands of cats,
Millions and billions and
Trillions of cats.

'Oh,' cried the old man joyfully, 'now I can choose the prettiest cat and take it home with me!' So he chose one. It was white.

But just as he was about to leave, he saw another one all black and white and it seemed just as pretty as the first. So he took this one also.

But then he saw a fuzzy grey kitten way over here which was every bit as pretty as the others so he took it too.

And now he saw one way down in a corner which he thought too lovely to leave so he took this too.

And just then, over here, the very old

man found a kitten which was black and very beautiful.

'It would be a shame to leave that one,' said the very old man. So he took it.

And now, over there, he saw a cat which had brown and yellow stripes like a baby tiger.

'I simply must take it!' cried the very old man, and he did.

So it happened that every time the very old man looked up, he saw another cat which was so pretty he could not bear to leave it, and before he knew it, he had chosen them all.

And so he went back over the sunny hills and down through the cool valleys, to show all his pretty kittens to the very old woman.

It was very funny to see those hundreds and thousands and millions and billions and trillions of cats following him.

They came to a pond.

'Mew, mew! We are thirsty!' cried the

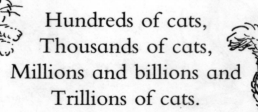

Hundreds of cats,
Thousands of cats,
Millions and billions and
Trillions of cats.

'Well, here is a great deal of water,' said the very old man.

Each cat took a sip of water, and the pond was gone!

'Mew, mew! Now we are hungry!' said the

Hundreds of cats,
Thousands of cats,
Millions and billions and
Trillions of cats.

'There is much grass on the hills,' said the very old man.

Each cat ate a mouthful of grass and not a blade was left!

Pretty soon the very old woman saw them coming.

'My dear!' she cried. 'What are you doing? I asked for one little cat, and what do I see?—

Cats here, cats there,
Cats and kittens everywhere,
Hundreds of cats,
Thousands of cats,
Millions and billions and
Trillions of cats.'

'But we can never feed them all,' said
the very old woman. 'They will eat us
out of house and home.'

'I never thought of that,' said the very
old man. 'What shall we do?'

The very old woman thought for a
while and then she said, 'I know! We

will let the cats decide which one we should keep.'

'Oh yes,' said the very old man, and he called to the cats. 'Which one of you is the prettiest?'

'I am!'

'I am!'

'No, I am!'

'No, I am the prettiest!'

'I am!'

'No, I am! I am! I am!' cried hundreds and thousands and millions and billions and trillions of voices, for each cat thought itself the prettiest.

And they began to quarrel.

They bit and scratched and clawed each other and made such a great noise that the very old man and the very old woman ran into the house as fast as they could. They did not like such quarrelling.

But after a while the noise stopped and the very old man and the very old woman peeped out of the window to see what had happened. They could not see a single cat!

'I think they must have eaten each other all up,' said the very old woman. 'It's too bad!'

'But look!' said the very old man, and he pointed to a bunch of high grass. In it sat one little frightened kitten. They went out and picked it up. It was thin and scraggly.

'Poor little kitty,' said the very old woman.

'Dear little kitty,' said the very old man, 'how does it happen that you were

not eaten up with all those hundreds
and thousands and millions and billions
and trillions of cats?'

'Oh, I'm just a very homely little cat,'
said the kitten, 'so when you asked who
was the prettiest I didn't say anything.
So nobody bothered about me.'

They took the kitten into the house, where the very old woman gave it a warm bath and brushed its fur until it was soft and shiny.

Every day they gave it plenty of milk – and soon it grew nice and plump.

'And it is a very pretty cat, after all!' said the very old woman.

'It is the most beautiful cat in the whole world,' said the very old man. 'I ought to know, for I've seen—

Hundreds of cats,
Thousands of cats,
Millions and billions and
Trillions of cats—

and not one is as pretty as this one.'

This story is by Wanda Gag.

The Rajah's Secret

The musical instruments play an important part and the 'joining-in' element is rhythmical. The story-teller introduces the rhythm by clapping it on reading 'Boom-boom, boom-boom, boom-boom' and encourages the listeners to join in with the clapping to the words 'The Rajah has big ears'.

i.e. Boom-boom / boom-boom / boom-boom
The Ra- / jah has / big ears

This is repeated with
Boom-boom / boom / boom / boom
Who told / the / sec- / ret?

and

Boom / boom!
Man- / ji!

The story can also be told, of course, with real instruments.

The Rajah's Secret

There was once a man who worked in the gardens of the palace of a great Rajah. This Rajah had a secret. Everyone knew he had a secret but no-one knew what it was. Every day, the great lord would walk in the palace gardens and all the servants would fall on their knees and hide their faces. Was it any wonder that he was a vain man?

One hot day, Manji, the gardener, was working in a tall tree near the palace walls when he found himself looking into an inner court. The Rajah was there. He saw the Rajah do something he had never seen him do before. He removed his grand headdress. And now, Manji knew the Rajah's secret!

The Rajah had big ears!

From that moment, Manji could not rest. He ached to tell the secret but he dared not. What if the Rajah found out? Manji feared for his life. But every day that he kept the secret to himself, the more difficult it became.

At last, he could bear it no longer. He rushed back to the tall old tree and threw his arms round it.

'I know the Rajah's secret,' he whispered. 'The Rajah has big ears!'

He felt as if a great weight had been lifted from him. He had told the secret but it would remain a secret, for only the tree knew.

In due course, the old tree was cut down. It was taken to the sawmill and the wood was bought by a craftsman who made musical instruments. The tree was gone. The secret was safe.

The Rajah held a great celebration and all the people were invited. There was more food than most of them had seen in a year, fireworks and music from the Rajah's own musicians. Indeed, the Royal Musician was most anxious to show everyone the splendid new

instruments he had bought: tabla, sitar
and flute. The Rajah commanded them
to begin.

They began to beat the tabla.

Boom-boom, boom-boom, boom-
boom
Boom-boom, boom-boom, boom-
boom

The gardener leaned forward. The
Rajah did, too. The drums seemed to
have a message.

The Rajah has big ears
The Rajah has big ears

The rhythm changed as the music
continued.

Boom-boom, boom, boom, boom
Boom-boom, boom, boom, boom

Who told the secret?
Who told the secret?

And as Manji grew more and more
frightened, the drums gave the answer.

Boom boom!
Boom boom!
Boom boom!

Manji!
Manji!
Manji!

The Rajah rose to his feet. He seemed
to Manji to grow taller and taller. He
gave a great roar of rage.

'Who is responsible for this?'

Manji ran to him and threw himself at his feet.

'I didn't tell anyone the secret,' he said. 'Truly, I only told the tree,' and he covered his face with his hands.

There was a long silence. When Manji dared at last to peep through his fingers, the Rajah seemed smaller, more like an ordinary man, and his face was very red.

'So you told the tree,' he said, more quietly, 'and the tree became the instruments and the instruments told my secret because they know nothing of the foolishness of men.' He sat down again, looking thoughtful.

'How stupid I have been,' he said, at last. 'And how hot and uncomfortable in this elaborate headdress,' and he tossed it on the ground. 'I forgive you, Manji. Let us hear these excellent new instruments again.' And the Royal

Musicians played while everyone
clapped and sang and laughed.

The Rajah has big ears
The Rajah has big ears

Who told the secret?
Who told the secret?

Manji!
Manji!

But because the Rajah had been wise
and kind, they now also sang

Our Rajah is a hero
Our Rajah is a hero
Hurrah! Hurrah! Hurrah!

*This is a re-telling by Pat Thomson of an
Indian folk tale.*

The Rat King's Daughter

On a first hearing, the first and last lines of the conversation tend to be picked up as the story proceeds. ('Why do you seek me, little brother?' and 'Then you are not fit to marry the Rat Princess! I must travel on.') On subsequent hearing, the listeners can be asked to take the part of the Rat King, responding to the Sun, the Cloud and the Great Wall.

The Rat King's Daughter

Far away and long ago, there was born a Rat Princess. Her father, the Rat King, and her mother, the Rat Queen, were full of happiness.

'She is the most beautiful princess under the stars,' declared the Rat King. 'She will marry no-one but the most powerful person in the world, let him live under, over or in the earth. I will see to that.'

When the time came for the Rat Princess to marry, *she* wanted to marry the Grey Rat who lived over the mountains but her father would not hear of it. He consulted his advisors, for he was determined that she would marry well. They thought, and considered, and then the old rat called Ancient and Wise said, 'The Sun is the most powerful. We feel his great power and, without him, the rice would never ripen. The Sun is the most powerful person in the world.'

So the Rat King set off on a journey to find the Sun. He travelled for many days until he came to the high mountains. He climbed higher and higher until one morning, he found the Sun.

'Why do you seek me, little brother?' asked the Sun.

'I come to offer you the hand of my daughter, the Rat Princess. Only you shall be her husband, for you are the most powerful person in the world.'

The Sun laughed. 'You are gracious, little brother, but I am not the most powerful person in the world. When the Cloud passes me, he hides me.'

'Then you are not fit to marry the Rat Princess! I must travel on.'

The Rat King journeyed until he found the Cloud, hanging low over the rice fields.

'Why do you seek me, little brother?'

'I come to offer you the hand of my daughter, the Rat Princess. Only you shall be her husband for you are the most powerful person in the world.'

'You are gracious, little brother, but I am not the most powerful person in the world. When the Wind blows, I must go where he sends me.'

'Then you are not fit to marry the Rat Princess! I must travel on.'

The Rat King journeyed until he found the Wind, sweeping through a green valley.

'Why do you seek me, little brother?'

'I come to offer you the hand of my daughter, the Rat Princess. Only you shall be her husband for you are the most powerful person in the world.'

'You are gracious, little brother, but as I blow across the land, I come to a Great Wall which never allows me to pass. I cannot be the most powerful person in the world.'

'Then you are not fit to marry the Rat Princess! I must travel on.'

The Rat King journeyed down the valley, across the plains and over the mountains until he came to the Great Wall, which was the Great Wall of China.

'Why do you seek me, little brother?'

'I come to offer you the hand of my daughter, the Rat Princess. Only you shall be her husband, for you are the most powerful person in the world.'

'You are gracious, little brother,' sighed the Great Wall, 'but I cannot be the most powerful person in the world.

Under my stones lives someone far more
powerful. He gnaws and gnaws at me
and one day, I shall crumble away to
nothing. You must ask the Grey Rat.'

And so, after all his long travels, the Rat King found the most powerful person in the world to marry his beautiful daughter.

And the Rat Princess was very happy indeed, for *she* had always intended to marry the handsome Grey Rat.

This story is a Chinese folk-tale re-told by Pat Thomson.

The Lion Hunt

The story-teller begins by instructing everyone to copy everything he/she says or does. The listeners then repeat every line after the teller, copying the noises and actions.

The Lion Hunt

Do you want to go on a Lion Hunt?
YES!

Follow me down the path.
   pat your thighs in a steady walking rhythm
The horses are ready.
   click tongue
Stop here.
   whoa, boy
We're going to walk across those fields,
   point ahead
through the forest to the mountains.
   point up
This is easy – short grass.
   swish hands together, briskly

106

Across the wooden bridge.
  thump chest
Through the long grass.
  swish hands together slowly
It's getting harder.
The wind's blowing up.
  blow
Now it's raining.
  rotate palms quickly
It's getting muddy.
  lift each foot while making slurping noises
There's a stream.
But no bridge!

Shall we take a run?
Here goes.
simulate jump by slapping thighs very fast,
pausing, then 'landing' with one loud slap
Phew! Made it!
We've disturbed the mosquitoes.
slap wildly (preferably oneself)
Into the forest.
We'll have to cut our way through.
appropriate hand movements whilst saying,
'chop, chop'

This is very hard work.
But we're near the top.
A bit further.
We're here.
WELL DONE, EVERYBODY!

Wait a minute.
What's that?
It's a cave.
It's very dark.
Can you feel anything?

(quietly)   There's something warm.
                It's something furry.

(loudly)   It's a LION!

*(Now go through the journey in reverse,
but very fast)*

Into the forest.
   chop, chop, chop
Swat those mosquitoes!
   slap, slap, slap
Jump over the stream.
   pat thighs fast, pause, and 'land'

Through the mud.
  slurp, slurp, slurp
Through the long grass.
  long swishes
Over the wooden bridge.
  thump chest
Through the short grass.
  quick swishes
Get back on the horses.
  click tongue
Stop here.
  whoa, boy
Quick, up the path to home.
  make running sound with hands on thighs
Phew!
  big sigh of relief

Do you want to go on a Lion Hunt?
NO!

*This story is a traditional story re-told by
Pat Thomson.*

The Night Troll

This is not a story which invites joining-in on a first hearing but it is a very enjoyable story to tell together when your listeners know it. The rhyming couplets are not difficult to remember and the variation between the voice of the composed girl and that of the fierce troll is relished.

The Night Troll

If you walk and walk until you come to
the furthest farm in the northernmost
country, you will find a huge stone in
the shape of a troll. I will tell you how
it came to be there.

It was Christmas Eve, and all the family were looking forward to making the long journey to church and meeting the neighbours. They rarely saw them during the rest of the year on the lonely farm. They would exchange greetings, eat well and celebrate. It would take them all day to get there, however, and they would have to stay overnight. This year, the smallest baby was too young to go on such a long, hard journey and someone would have to stay behind to look after her. But no-one wanted to stay behind, and there was a good reason for that. You see, on Christmas Eve, the night troll would come down the mountain and visit the farm and, if you valued your life, you made sure you were not there on Christmas Eve.

In the past, there had been one or two foolish enough to remain alone at the farm on this special night and they had been found stiff and dead, or never found again at all.

Now, there was one person in the family who was brave enough to remain: the eldest girl. She thought she might be able to manage a troll. She knew that they like the sound of their own voices and cannot bear not to have the last word. She also knew that you must never look at them directly and that their power disappears at sunrise. She said she would stay behind.

At first, all was quiet. The baby had her supper and the girl sang her to sleep. Then, although she tried to keep awake, gradually she grew sleepier and sleepier.

She was awakened by the baby's whimpers. The sound of heavy feet stamping on the turf outside told her that the troll was coming. She sat very still. Someone was breathing loudly outside the window. Wood splintered as the shutters were torn off and long nails scratched at the glass. She knew the troll was behind her, looking in through the window. She picked up the baby and, keeping her back to the troll, began to rock her to the rhythm of a song.

Sleep little baby, do not cry.
Your sister is singing a lullaby.

She sang quietly, and nearly jumped out of her skin as the troll joined in loudly with his own words.

Human girl, your eyes are blue.
Look at me. Mine are, too.

The girl continued to rock the baby and did not even glance in his direction, but she went on:

Horrid troll, close your eyes,
Do not disturb my lullabies.

The troll rattled the window panes and

growled angrily.

> Human, your hands are soft and
>   weak.
> Look at mine, so hard and quick.

The girl still would not look. She rocked
the baby and sang back:

> Horrid troll, your hands do harm.
> Go away and leave this farm.

The troll roared and banged on the
window. The girl thought she heard the
sound of glass cracking, but she refused
to show she was frightened and tapped
her foot gently as she sang. The troll
shouted:

> Little feet tapping to your song.
> Look at mine, so big and strong.

The girl looked straight ahead, never

turning, and quickly replied:

If they're as handsome as you say,
Use them now, to trip away.

The troll was in a rage. He shrieked. He
ran to the door and burst it open. Still
the girl did not turn. She went on
singing quietly to the baby. The troll
lowered his voice and spoke urgently, to
trick her.

Look over your shoulder. Turn
     around.
There's something marvellous I have
     found.

On her back, through the open door,
the girl felt the warmth of the winter sun
and replied:

You speak the truth. A marvel is here.
Look over *your* shoulder, troll, my
     dear.

The troll turned round and saw the sun rising, flooding the land with light. And as he watched, he turned to stone.

If you walk and walk, until you come to the furthest farm in the northernmost country, you will find the troll stone outside the farmhouse still.

This is a traditional Icelandic folktale, retold by Pat Thomson.

Ticky Picky Boom Boom

All that is needed for this story is a quick
rehearsal of

Ticky picky boom boom
Ticky picky boom boom
Ticky picky boom boom BOUF!

To add to the fun, suggest that everyone pats
their knees as they say it to suggest that the
yams are on the march.

Ticky Picky Boom Boom

Ananse the trickster had a very fine vegetable garden. He had every vegetable imaginable; plenty of potatoes and more yams than he could eat. But there was one thing he did not have: a flower garden, and Ananse wanted above all to have flowers, just like a rich man.

'I shall turn the yam patch into a flower garden,' he decided, 'and I shall make Mr Tiger dig the flower bed for me.'

Now Mr Tiger had been tricked by Ananse before and he was cautious.

'What will you give me if I dig out the yams?' he asked.

'You may keep all the yams you dig up,' replied Ananse.

Mr Tiger was satisfied with that. He loved to eat yams. So, early next morning, he began to dig Ananse's garden for him. All day, he dug and dug, but the harder he worked, the deeper the yams seemed to sink into the ground. By the end of the day, Ananse's garden was thoroughly turned over, but Mr Tiger had not been able to get any yams for himself at all.

Mr Tiger was hot, tired and furious. This was another of Ananse's tricks! He lost his temper and chopped at one of the yams. He chopped it into little pieces, and then set off for home, muttering angrily.

What was that?

Behind him, Mr Tiger heard a noise. A shuffling noise at first and then a

126

stamping of small feet. Mr Tiger turned around – and along the road behind him, walking on little vegetable legs, came the yams! The noise that their feet made went like this:

Ticky picky boom boom
Ticky picky boom boom
Ticky picky boom boom bouf!

Tiger began to run.
The yams began to run, too.
Tiger began to gallop.
The yams began to gallop.
Tiger jumped.
The yams jumped.

Mr Tiger made straight for Mr Dog's house, running as fast as he could.

'Brother Dog,' he shouted, 'hide me! The yams are coming.'

'All right,' said Brother Dog. 'Hide behind me but don't say a word.'

So Mr Tiger hid behind Dog.

And down the road came the yams
and the noise that their feet made
sounded like this:

Ticky picky boom boom
Ticky picky boom boom
Ticky picky boom boom bouf!

The yams said, 'Brother Dog, have
you seen Mr Tiger?'

And Brother Dog looked straight ahead and said, 'I can't see Mr Tiger anywhere, not at all.'

But Mr Tiger was so frightened that he called out, 'Don't tell them, Brother Dog!' and Dog was so cross that he ran off and left Mr Tiger to the yams.

And the yams jumped.
And Tiger jumped.
And the yams ran.
And Tiger ran.
And the yams galloped.
And Tiger galloped.

Then Mr Tiger saw Sister Duck and all her little ducklings, so he hurried up to her and said, 'Sister Duck, hide me! The yams are coming!'

'All right,' said Sister Duck. 'Get behind me but don't say a word.'

So Mr Tiger hid behind Sister Duck. And down the road came the yams, and the noise that their feet made sounded like this:

131

Ticky picky boom boom
Ticky picky boom boom
Ticky picky boom boom bouf!

The yams said, 'Sister Duck, have you seen Mr Tiger?'

And Sister Duck looked straight ahead and said, 'Well now, I can't see him anywhere. Nowhere at all.'

But Mr Tiger was so frightened he shouted out, 'Don't tell them, Sister Duck,' and Sister Duck was so cross that she moved away and left him to the yams.

And the yams jumped.

And Tiger jumped.

And the yams ran.

And Tiger ran.

And the yams galloped.

And Tiger galloped.

He galloped and galloped, but he was getting tired, and still he could hear the yams coming along the road behind him, getting nearer and nearer. At last, he came to a stream and over the stream was a little plank bridge. On the other side was Mr Goat.

Mr Tiger ran across the bridge and called out, 'Mr Goat, hide me! The yams are coming!'

'All right,' said Mr Goat, 'but don't say a word.'

So Mr Tiger hid behind Mr Goat.

And down the road came the yams, and the noise that their feet made sounded like this:

Ticky picky boom boom
Ticky picky boom boom
Ticky picky boom boom bouf!

When they reached the bridge, they called out, 'Mr Goat, have you seen Mr Tiger?'

And Mr Goat looked straight ahead but before he could say anything, Mr Tiger shouted, 'Don't tell them, Mr Goat, don't tell them.'

The yams jumped on to the bridge but so did Mr Goat, and he just put down his head and butted them into the stream. Then Mr Goat and Mr Tiger picked the pieces out of the water and took them home to make a great feast of yams. But they certainly did *not* invite Ananse to the feast.

When the nights are dark, Mr Tiger stays at home. He dare not walk along the road, for behind him, he still thinks he hears a noise which sounds like this:

Ticky picky boom boom
Ticky picky boom boom
Ticky picky boom boom bouf!

This is an Ananse story told by Pat Thomson.

Author's Note

The stories about Ananse the trickster spider come from the West Indies and Africa. This particular one comes from Jamaica.

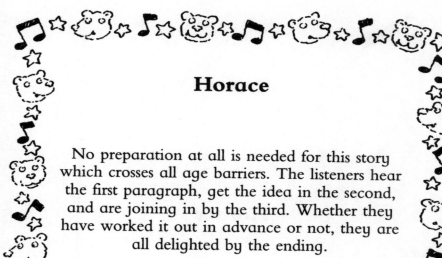

Horace

No preparation at all is needed for this story which crosses all age barriers. The listeners hear the first paragraph, get the idea in the second, and are joining in by the third. Whether they have worked it out in advance or not, they are all delighted by the ending.

Horace

Once upon a time there was a family
who all lived together in a little house in
a wood. There was—
　　Great-Grandpa,
　　Great-Grandma,
　　Grandpa,
　　Grandma,
　　Pa,
　　Ma,
　　Paul,
　　and little Lulu.
And with them lived HORACE.
Horace was a bear!

One day, Pa went out hunting, and on the way back he was met by—
Great-Grandma,
Grandpa,
Grandma,
Ma,
Paul,
and little Lulu.

And they all said, 'What do you think has happened?'

And Pa said, 'What *has* happened?'

And they said, 'Horace has eaten Great-Grandpa!'

And Pa was just WILD, and he said,
'I will KILL Horace!'

But they all took on so, he hadn't the
heart to do it.

And the next day, Pa went out hunting,
and on the way back he was met by—

    Grandpa,

    Grandma,

    Ma,

    Paul,

    and little Lulu.

And they all said, 'What do you think has happened?'

And Pa said, 'What *has* happened?'

And they said, 'Horace has eaten Great-Grandma!'

And Pa was just WILD, and he said, 'I will KILL Horace!'

But they all took on so, he hadn't the heart to do it.

And the next day, Pa went out hunting, and on the way back he was met by—

Grandma,

Ma,

Paul,

and little Lulu.

And they all said, 'What do you think has happened?'

And Pa said, 'What *has* happened?'

And they all said, 'Horace has eaten Grandpa!'

And Pa was just WILD, and he said, 'I will KILL Horace!'

But they all took on so, he hadn't the heart to do it.

And the next day, Pa went out hunting, and on the way back he was met by—
Ma,
Paul,
and little Lulu.
And they all said, 'What do you think has happened?'
And Pa said, 'What *has* happened?'
And they said, 'Horace has eaten Grandma!'
And Pa was just WILD, and he said, 'I will KILL Horace!'
But they all took on so, he hadn't the heart to do it.

And the next day, Pa went out hunting, and on the way back he was met by—
Paul,
and little Lulu.

And they both said, 'What do you think has happened?'

And Pa said, 'What *has* happened?'

And they said, 'Horace has eaten Ma!'

And Pa was just WILD, and he said, 'I will KILL Horace!'

But they all took on so, he hadn't the heart to do it.

And the next day, Pa went out hunting, and on the way back he was met by little Lulu.

And little Lulu said, 'What do you think has happened?'

And Pa said, 'What *has* happened?'

And little Lulu said, 'Horace has eaten Paul!'

And Pa was just WILD, and he said, 'I will KILL Horace!'

But little Lulu took on so, he hadn't the heart to do it.

And the next day, Pa went out hunting, and on the way back he was met by Horace.

And Horace said, 'What do you think has happened?'

And Pa said, 'What *has* happened?'

And Horace said, 'I've eaten little Lulu!'

And Pa was just WILD, and he said, 'I will KILL you, Horace!'

But Horace took on so, he hadn't the heart to do it.

And the next day, Horace went out hunting.

This story is by Alice B. Coats.